Groovy Girls™
Sleep Over Club

The Great Outdoors
Take a Hike

Robin Epstein

Scholastic Inc.

New York Toronto London Auckland Sydney
Mexico City New Delhi Hong Kong Buenos Aires

Read all the books about the Groovy Girls!

To Linda,
a BFF and adventurer who's always been a trailblazer

Cover illustration by Taia Morley

Interior illustrations by Yancey Labat and Steven Lee Stinnett

ISBN 0-439-81436-7

© 2005 Manhattan Group, LLC
All rights reserved. Published by Scholastic Inc.
SCHOLASTIC, LITTLE APPLE, and associated logos are trademarks
and/or registered trademarks of Scholastic Inc.

The Groovy Girls™ books are produced under license from Manhattan Group, LLC.
Go to groovygirls.com for more Groovy Girls fun!

12 11 10 9 8 7 6 5 4 3 2 1   6 7 8 9 10/0

Printed in the U.S.A.
First Little Apple printing, September 2005

Chapter 1

Are We There Yet?

"This is like a snow day—only better!" Gwen said between happy bites of the peanut butter 'n' fluff sandwich she was eating for breakfast that morning (but was supposed to be saving for lunch that afternoon!).

"I love, love, love field trips," Reese replied to her best friend, Gwen, as they stared out the window of their school bus, bound for Happy Trails State Park. "But snow days are great, too."

Gwen waved to the truck driver in the next lane. **HONK! HOOOOOOOONK! HONK!** the trucker responded.

"But you don't get *that* on a snow day!" Gwen giggled.

"Yeah!" O'Ryan nodded at her twin, Reese. "Gwen's totally right."

"Thank you," Gwen said, and just as she started to stand up to take a bow, the bus made a hard left turn.

"WHOA!!!" everyone shouted as people started sliding in their seats.

And then *"WHOA!!!"* they shouted again as the bus righted itself, and they slid back in the other direction. "EEEEEP!" Gwen squealed, landing in Reese's lap.

"I believe that was the sound of a Gwen-bird," Vanessa said, turning to her BFF, Yvette.

Yvette put her hand to her forehead, as if she were trying to spot this exotic bird herself. "Yup," she replied, "I bee-lieve you're right, Nessa. And the 'Gwen' is a very rare bird. I mean, can you imagine if there were more than one of them?!"

"Well, I think two Gwen-birds would be twice as nice!" Reese replied.

"EEEEEP, EEEEEP, EEEEP!" Gwen cheeped, flapping her arms to the giggles of her friends.

As the bus continued to bounce around, the bouncier its passengers got too! In fact, the feeling of excitement on that school bus was as catchy as a pop song.

"Good-day, sunshine, duh-nuh-nuh," Yvette sang. "Good-night, moon time, duh-nuh-nuh!"

"Go fish!" O'Ryan exclaimed. "Hey, I said, 'go fish,' Oki," she added, trying to snap her best friend back into the game they'd been playing.

"You guys brought cards?" Vanessa asked, turning her attention across the aisle.

"Yep," O'Ryan said. "Since we're going to the great outdoors, I thought we should warm up by playing Go Fish."

"Hellllloooo," Gwen replied. "You *do* know

we're going to a park and *not* an aquarium, riiiiight?"

"That's why I loaded my iPod with songs from bands called The Byrds and the Beastie Boys," Vanessa chimed in. "I mean, when you're in the woods, you gotta do like the animals do, right?"

The field trippers had been told to pack a lunch, and they knew they'd be getting a Happy Trails map to navigate the park once they arrived. But this still left plenty of room in their backpacks for extra goodies.

"Guess what I packed in my sack," Gwen said to all her friends.

"Give us a hint," Reese replied. "After all, we're going to be getting clues when they send us out to find stuff in the park. It'll be good practice."

"Okay," Gwen answered. "Here's your hint: What I've got in my backpack goes with a hug and wears an aluminum-foil coat."

The girls thought about the clue for a moment. What went with a hug? And was dressed in foil?

"A Kiss!" Reese said, puckering her lips. "You brought Hershey's Kisses, didn't you? Now, why doesn't that surprise me?"

"Because I'm a pretty sweet treat myself!" Gwen exclaimed.

"Speaking of which," Oki said, "I brought vanilla-scented hand cream, if anyone wants some. And I also brought a bottle of spray mist to keep our faces fresh. And a bag of Clementines that we can all have for a snack. And—"

"Don't you think that's gonna be a *lot* to carry around all day?" Vanessa asked. "Oranges are heavy, even if they're the little kind."

"I don't mind," Oki replied.

"But it might slow us down," Vanessa said. "I mean, this isn't just some stroll through the woods we're taking."

Truth be told, Oki *had* been thinking of their nature hike as more of a stroll. But even after Vanessa reminded her of their mission— they needed to be like treasure hunters using their map skills—Oki couldn't imagine how vanilla-scented hand cream could be anything but a good thing!

"Vanessa's right!" Yvette added. "When pirates went looking for buried treasure, they probably didn't carry lotion on board."

"No duh," Oki replied, not to be outdone. "Because what would Captain Hook have done with hand lotion anyway?"

"Well, just remember," Vanessa added, "we want to get through the park as fast as we can so we can get back to the bus before any of the other teams."

"I don't think that's exactly the point of the field trip, Vanessa," Reese said. "I think Mrs. Pearlman wants us to explore the park, enjoy nature, and work on our map skills."

"Yeah, so we can show that we've learned all that snoozy stuff in class!" Oki added.

"Right!" O'Ryan nodded. "Like 'Never Eat Shredded Wheat!'"

"Why not?" Yvette asked. "Are you allergic?"

"She's not allergic!" Oki replied. "'Never Eat Shredded Wheat' is the way we were taught to remember directions."

"What does shredded wheat have to do with finding your way anywhere?" Vanessa asked. "Unless you're trying to find your way out of a cereal box."

"Never stands for north," Oki said. "Eat is for east. Shredded is for south. And Wheat is for west. So if you think of a compass like a clock, north is always at 12 o'clock. Since east always comes next, it goes where 3 o'clock is. South is next, and since it's directly opposite of north, it goes in the 6 o'clock spot. Then there's west, which is directly opposite east, so you know that's at 9 o'clock."

"Wow," Gwen laughed. "And all I remembered from that lesson was how much I didn't like shredded wheat. But as long as I've got my trusty Kisses, I'm good to go!"

And sure enough, when the bus pulled into the parking lot, Gwen was the first of the Groovies to rush off the bus, powered by the thrill of the adventure that lay ahead and, of course, a handful of Kisses.

Chapter 2

The Countdown Begins!

"**S**cuse me! 'Scuse me! Coming through!" Vanessa yelled, pushing to get up to the front of the Happy Trails State Park sign, where the group leaders were gathering.

As Vanessa marched by the twins to pick up their team's park map and "creativity kits"—one for each girl—Reese and O'Ryan exchanged a look. It was a look that said, *Yeah, we probably would have made her our hike leader, but it would have been nice if she had asked us first!*

"Good, all 25 teams are present and accounted for," Mrs. Pearlman announced to everyone. "And no team has more than six members, right?"

"How lucky are we that there are exactly six of us?" Gwen said. "What would we have done if there had been another Groovy Girl?"

"Vanessa would have worked it out," Yvette nodded. "'Cause my best friend, V, is as sharp as deli mustard!"

Oki leaned forward to sneak a peek at one of the creativity kits. "What's all that in there?"

"Looks like a bright orange cap and a garbage bag," O'Ryan said, shaking her head. "A bright orange cap for a girl with red hair! I mean, how am I ever going to use that?"

"And a garbage bag?" Oki said. "That's not so cool either."

"It's cool if you're a garbage collector!" Reese replied. "But look, I think I see walkie-talkies in there too."

"Walkie-talkies? Yippee!" Gwen exclaimed, putting an "air-walkie" up to her mouth and speaking into her hand. "Ten-four, good buddy, this is Gwen-bird on Happy Trail. Do you read me?"

"The walkie-talkies are to be used *only* in emergency situations," Mrs. Pearlman said, nodding at Gwen. "Do you read me?"

"Ten-four," Gwen said back.

"Okay, now who can remind me of the rules of our treasure hunt today?" Mrs. Pearlman asked.

"We take the envelope with our group name on it," Reese shouted out, "read the clue inside, go where it tells us to, and then do whatever it is we're supposed to do there. Then we find our next envelope and move on to the next place."

"Good," Mrs. P. replied. "What else is important to keep in mind as you explore the park?"

"We're supposed to use the stuff in our creativity kits creatively," Yvette said, "and finish as many tasks as we can before 2 p.m. 'cause that's when we need to get back on the bus."

"Right, Yvette, and there will be a total of three envelopes to find. But," Mrs. P. said, "you'll be asked to complete four tasks along the way. How's that possible?"

"One of them must be a two-parter!" Vanessa shouted.

"See that?" Yvette said, turning to Gwen. "Told you she was sharp."

"So if we can't figure out where to go," Oki said, raising her pointer finger, "all we have to do is follow the trail of teams in front of us, right?"

"Now how's that for being one sharp cheddar?" O'Ryan exclaimed, proudly nodding at her best friend.

"Aha, clever idea, Oki!" Mrs. P. replied. "But we've pre-assigned different starting destinations so you'll all be scattered."

"Dagnabbit," Oki said. "Guess someone's more cleverer than me!"

"But you were using your noodle," Mrs. P. replied, pointing to her head. "And that instinct is key."

"Speaking of noodles," Gwen whispered to Reese, "when's lunch?"

"We haven't even started the hike yet," Reese

whispered back. "And besides, you've already eaten yours!"

"A couple more things to tell you before you go," Mrs. Pearlman said. "You'll all be relying on your map skills, your creativity, your resourcefulness, and one another today, but teachers and parent monitors will be in the park just in case you need them. And members of the top three finishing teams will get extra credit points to use any way they like when we're back in class. Last thing: What time must everyone be back on the bus?"

"TWO P.M.!" everyone shouted.

"Seems like we're playing 'Beat the Clock'!" Gwen said.

"A little bit," Mrs. P. replied. "Now, please synchronize your watches. The time is exactly 11:45 A.M. You have precisely 2 hours and 15 minutes to complete your tasks. Good luck, have fun...and...GO!"

When Mrs. P. blew her whistle, the group leaders dashed to find their first envelopes, which had been scattered beneath the pine needles under a nearby tree.

Vanessa quickly found **Groovy Girls Group Envelope #1** and jogged back to her team as fast as she could.

Groovy Girls Group
Envelope #1

"Lay it on us, Vanessa!" Gwen clapped. "And read fast—I need all the extra credit I can get!"

"Okay," Vanessa said, ripping open the envelope and finding this clue inside:

Before beginning any journey, it's always smart to stop here first.

Rearrange this word jumble to spell out your destination. When you've figured out both words, put them together to form one word.

TOU SHOEU

"Tou?" Yvette repeated. "Shoeu?"

"Wait, there's more," Vanessa said, reading the bottom of the card:

14

> Proceed 400 yards north of the Happy Trails State Park sign to arrive at this destination.

"Four *hundred* yards!" Gwen yelped. "That's, like, a mile or something."

"Wait, no!" Reese said. "It's not nearly that far. Just think about running the 100-yard dash."

"Ooh, I hate thinking about that!" Gwen said.

"I mean, just picture the distance we run outside during gym class," Reese continued. "Then, like, multiply it by four."

"Oh, okay, got it!" Gwen said. "So it's not *that* far, but...but where is it?"

"Well, I can tell you *that* as soon as we figure out what direction north is," O'Ryan said. "Let's see that map, Vanessa."

"C'mon, let's just start walking!" Gwen said, pounding on her watch. "We're losing time."

"Gwen, we have to know where we're going first," Oki replied.

"Well, I say we just go that-a-way!" Gwen pointed, and started walking.

"Gwen, wait, no!" Vanessa yelled.

"Why?" Gwen replied, stopping in her tracks.

"Well," Vanessa said, "because I'm the leader and," she continued—realizing a strong leader needed to take control early or risk losing it—"and my gut instinct tells me we need to go that-a-way." Vanessa then pointed in exactly the *opposite* direction that Gwen was headed.

"I think we should follow Vanessa," Yvette nodded, "'cause the girl's got a lot of guts. And *she's* our leader!"

"Well, I think we'll figure out the *right* way to go as soon we get ourselves oriented with this map," O'Ryan said.

"Yeah," Oki nodded. "We just need to find the Happy Trails State Park sign on the map, 'cause that's where we're standing right now, then look at the compass to show us where north is."

The compass rose was on the bottom part of the map, and it gave all four directions.

But as Oki and O'Ryan were busy angling the map, and as Vanessa stood there tapping her foot, the time clock kept ticking.

Tick…

Tick…

Tick…

Tick…

Tick…

Tick…

Until all of a sudden, "Outhouse! Outhouse! We're going to the outhouse!" Gwen started shouting.

The girls all looked over to Gwen with puzzled expressions on their faces.

"Tou Shoeu," she said excitedly. "Unjumbled it's O U T H O U S E. Just like it says on that sign."

Gwen pointed to a sign showing a little house with the word OUTHOUSE printed on top.

Beneath the picture, it even read 400 YARDS, with an arrow pointing in the direction she was headed.

"My extra credit, people!" Gwen said, starting to run. "Come on!"

It was hard to deny that Gwen was onto something, so when Vanessa nodded, the whole Groovy Group took off, dashing behind her.

With their packs jangling on their backs, all the Groovies were out of breath by the time they arrived at the site.

"What a cute little house!" Oki said, as she gulped the cool air. "And it looks just like its picture."

"Wonder who lives here," O'Ryan said, wiping the sweat from her brow.

"Whew," Yvette replied. "I don't know, but whoever it is, I hope they have a couch we can sit down on for a minute. I hate dashing!"

When the door to that outhouse swung open, though, the girls started laughing. Not only was there no couch in that house, the only piece of "furniture" it contained was a toilet.

Turned out outhouse was just a fancy way of saying "WC"…

Which was really a fancy way of saying "Water Closet"…

Which was a fancy way of saying "bathroom"!

"Are we really in the right place?" Oki asked O'Ryan.

"We sure are in the right place," Reese answered, "because next to that YOU ARE HERE sign over there is **Groovy Girls Group Envelope #2!**"

Vanessa walked up to the sign, grabbed the envelope, and ripped it open. "Okay, girls," she said, reading over the clue. "Let me see that map, O'Ryan."

"Map?" Gwen repeated. "Um, as I think I just proved to you guys, we don't need to waste time reading directions. We didn't need them to find the outhouse. So why should we need 'em now?"

Vanessa looked at her teammates, then looked at her watch.

They *had* made excellent time on the first task. And the only thing that had slowed them down was when Oki and O'Ryan were trying to orient themselves on the map.

Vanessa glanced back at Gwen, who put her hands on her hips.

"Tick, tick, tick, tick, tick," Gwen ticked.

"Okay," Vanessa said, making an executive decision. "Let's boogie, Groovies!"

And with that instruction, the Groovy Girls leap-frogged deeper into the woods.

Chapter 3

Over the River

12:17 P.M.

Part I:

From the outhouse, travel northwest to cross the stream where the water doesn't have to cross your shoes.

"Just take a flying leap!" Vanessa said.

"*You* take a flying leap!" Oki replied, standing at the stream the girls were now supposed to cross.

Thanks to Gwen, who'd luckily spotted the stream ahead of them—without even eyeing the map or thinking about the directions—the girls had, indeed, made their way to the water.

Naturally, this made Gwen feel pretty proud of herself. And she was trying hard not to gloat.

"I'd like to thank my mother for making me eat carrots to improve my eyesight," Gwen said, sounding like she was giving an acceptance speech at the Oscars. "Because, thanks to my perfect vision, we got here lickety-split!"

(Well, maybe Gwen wasn't trying *that* hard not to gloat.)

Now that they were at the stream, though, the other girls were beginning to see that Gwen's perfect vision might have led to one little problem: There was no way they could cross the stream without getting their tootsies soaked!

"Vanessa," O'Ryan said, "no matter how much air we catch while jumping, we can't make it across without going calf-deep in the water."

"Yeah, remember," Oki added, "we're s'posed to go to the place *'where the water doesn't have to cross your shoes.'"*

"So, uh, what now?" Yvette asked, looking to Vanessa.

Vanessa reread the clue card and realized that O'Ryan and Oki were probably right. And she knew as their leader, she needed to come up with a plan.

"Well, if you *don't* think we should cross the stream here," Vanessa asked, "what *do* you think we should do?"

"We should use the map to find the narrowest part of the stream," Oki said, "then cross there."

Sure enough, when Oki and O'Ryan studied the map, they soon spotted a location where it would be easy to hop-scotch across the stream— north and west of the outhouse—and just *exactly* where the clue card had told them to go!

"Now let's start walking till we find where we were supposed to have gone in the first place," O'Ryan said.

"But you can't even *see* a skinnier part of the stream from here. And if *I* can't see it, that means it's probably way far away," Gwen said. "Walking there will take too long. We'll lose too much time!"

"But my way's the dry way!" O'Ryan replied.

"Aw, c'mon, you'll barely get wet jumping across," Gwen said. "Look girls, the more time we spend here la-dee-dahing about this, the more time we lose! Tick. Tick. Tick. Tick. Tick."

"Would you stop with the tick-tocking!" Oki replied. "'Cause first of all, Gwen, we're off course. And second of all, no way am I tromping through *any* amount of water in my beautiful new suede shoes!"

The girls looked down at Oki's feet.

"I mean, would *you* want to put these puppies in water?" she asked, before holding out each leg to model her footgear.

Oki first lifted her right foot to show the girls, but as she lifted her left foot, she started to fall.

"Whooooaaaa!" Oki shouted as she tripped over a rock by the bank of the stream.

O'Ryan rushed over to help her friend back up, but as she was giving Oki a hand, she got an idea.

"*That's* how we can get across the stream without getting our feet wet!" she exclaimed, pointing to the rock. "We can put big rocks down, one in front of the other, so we can create a bridge across the stream. We'll stand on one rock and put the next down in front of it and then the next and the next and the next."

Vanessa weighed the options, then nodded. "Okay," she said. "Now hear this: Everyone collect two big rocks so we can lay out a good path."

"This is so *not* going to save us time!" Gwen whispered to Reese as the two girls went off in search of their rocks. "We're falling behind!"

"I don't know," Reese answered, as she picked up a large stone. "I mean, on the one hand you're right. We're definitely losing time by building a bridge."

"We sure are," Gwen nodded.

"But on the other hand," Reese continued, finding another rock and balancing out her load, "if we'd spent the time looking at the map earlier, we wouldn't have had to worry about this at all. We probably would have even found the skinny part of the stream and crossed it by now."

Gwen didn't have a response to this. So instead, she pretended like she hadn't heard it and walked away from Reese in search of big stones of her own.

"I can't believe how wrong my outfit is for today," Oki said to O'Ryan, zippering up her fleecy vest, as they hunted for their rocks.

O'Ryan looked at Oki, who now had dirt on her pleated skirt. "But you *do* look outrageously cute," O'Ryan said, trying to make her friend feel better while patting some of the dirt off Oki's skirt. "And, like you've always said, 'Looking right can never be wrong.'"

"Hey!" Yvette called out. "Vanessa wants us to scramble like eggs. So hurry up!"

Oki rolled her eyes.

But, quick as they could, the girls ran back to the edge of the stream with their rocks. Vanessa then took the first rock and placed it in the water.

"Okay," she said, stepping on top of the stone. "Someone hand me the next one."

Reese hoisted another large stone and passed

it to Vanessa, who then put it in front of the first and took a step forward. "Good," she said, "and now the next one."

The girls repeated the process—hand off, plop down, step lively, hand off, plop down, step lively—until Vanessa and the bridge reached the other side of the stream.

"Red rover, red rover, please come over!" Vanessa shouted.

Extending their arms out for balance, the rest of the Groovy Girls carefully walked across that stone path, imagining they were trapeze artists.

"Yipes!" Yvette exclaimed, as she felt herself starting to totter.

"Whatever you do," Reese yelled to Yvette, "don't picture yourself falling into the water!"

"Thanks a lot!" Yvette said, immediately picturing herself floating downstream. But proceeding with even greater caution, Yvette and the rest of the girls made it safely to the other side, where they kicked up their (dry) heels!

"Great teamwork, girls!" Vanessa said. "Great creative use of brainpower, too."

"Part one is done," Yvette nodded in response.

"But hot tamale, look at the time!" Reese said, after glancing at her watch. "It's 12:53 P.M.!"

ZOINKS!

"So teamwork and creativity were good," O'Ryan replied, "but maybe map-reading and direction-following would have been better."

"We only have 67 minutes left!" Vanessa said.

The girls' mouths dropped open. But there was no time to say anything more!

Chapter 4
A Sticky Situation

Part 2:

Now that you've gone over the "river," it's time to go through the woods.

You're not going to Grandmother's house, but if you were, wouldn't it be nice to bring her some fresh sap to make maple syrup?

Head to the part of the park that you can see from your map is most west of where you are now. There you'll find a grove of maple trees. Tap one of those trees and bring a cup of maple sap back to the bus with you.

12:55 P.M. – 65 minutes left

"What?" Reese asked, scratching her head after rereading the clue.

Gwen shrugged her shoulders. "Got me," she replied.

Gwen had lost some steam at the stream and decided to let the others take the lead on this one.

"Well, we can't just stand here," Vanessa said, as she stood by watching Oki and O'Ryan trace their fingers over the map.

"You have a plan?" Yvette asked, nodding at Vanessa.

"Of course I have a plan," Vanessa replied. "Not only am I group leader, but I've vacationed in Vermont."

"*And?*" O'Ryan asked.

"And," said Vanessa, "I know how to spot a maple tree. They were all over the place in Vermont."

"*So?*" Oki asked.

"So," Vanessa continued, "as soon as I see one of those trees, I'll recognize it, and we'll be able to tap its sap." As Vanessa was saying this, she was even beginning to convince herself. "Yeah," she continued, "*and so*, my way will be much faster than finding a whole grove of the trees 'cause we really only need one anyway."

"Well, that makes sense," Yvette replied.

"Now you're thinking like I'm thinking!" Gwen said, her enthusiasm quickly returning. "So let's make like a ball and bounce!"

1:04 P.M. – 56 minutes left

But even though Vanessa, Yvette, and Gwen had started walking, Oki, O'Ryan, and Reese had stayed where they were, continuing to inspect the map.

"Hey, Reese!" Gwen called back, "aren't you coming?"

Reese looked up at Gwen, but she didn't know what to do. On the one hand, she wanted to follow her best friend the way Yvette was following Vanessa. But on the other hand, she knew O'Ryan and Oki's plan made more sense.

"Well," Reese replied. "I think—"

"We got it!" O'Ryan shouted. "We know *exactly* where we need to go."

"We've charted the fastest course to the grove, no doubt about it," Oki confirmed. "And according to this map, it's up a hill and you girls are going in the wrong direction."

When the others saw Oki and O'Ryan's course— saw that there was even a classic maple leaf symbol (showing the five-pointed leaf) on the key—Yvette felt a little silly.

Yvette always gave Vanessa the benefit of the doubt. She thought that's what friends were supposed to do! But in this case, it seemed her pal and leader had things totally wardsback, or backwards.

"What do you think, Ness?" Yvette asked.

"Well, if that's what they think the map shows…okay," Vanessa replied.

"Okay, then," O'Ryan said when she realized everyone was finally on board with them. "Let's motor! Walk this way, please."

O'Ryan began taking zig-zag steps, which the rest of Team Groovy followed. And when she switched into a gallop, they trotted close behind.

The Groovies moved and grooved as quick as they could up that hill, but at a certain point, Oki stopped. Even though the temperature was quite cold, she'd started huffing and puffing like the big bad wolf.

"Guys, hang on a sec, my knapsack weighs a ton—I have to get rid of some of this stuff," she admitted. "Who wants a Clementine?"

"Ooh," Gwen replied, "that reminds me. I have some Kisses to share, too." But when she reached into her bag, all Gwen pulled out was a handful of chocolate goo! "EWWWW!" she said. "Look what happened to my sweet, sweet Kisses!"

Those chocolate Kisses had melted in the sun, just like a snowman in spring-time!

"No worries, Gwen," Reese said with a smile, "we'll help you eat up what hasn't melted yet."

"So does this mean no one wants one of my Clementines?" When Oki got no response, she added, "Well, good thing these babies are biodegradable." Because they were biodegradable, Oki knew if she left pieces of the oranges and their peels on the ground, they would eventually dissolve back into the earth, without causing harm to the environment.

"Um, I don't think you're supposed to do that," Reese said, as Oki peeled and dumped sections of her Clementines.

"Well, normally I wouldn't," Oki replied, as the girls kept trekking toward the cluster of maple trees. "But we *are* in nature, after all, so I'm acting like an animal!"

"Listen! You can hear some of the other teams in the distance. They're probably a lot farther along than us," Vanessa said, shaking her head. "You know," she whispered to Yvette, "if we'd followed *my* plan, I'm sure we would've already found a maple tree by now."

Yvette nodded, not knowing how else to

respond, since she wasn't sure anymore that V was such an authority on the woods. "How are we gonna get the sap out of the tree once we find it?" she asked instead, changing the subject.

"Well, I could tell you," Vanessa replied, "but maybe we should let O'Ryan and Oki try to explain it, since they seem so sure about everything else out here!"

"Um," O'Ryan replied, "Oki?"

"Reese knows, doesn't she?" Oki responded.

All eyes turned to Reese.

"No clue," Reese said, shaking her head. "Maybe it drips off the branches or something? But that's just a guess."

"I'm bummed you don't know, but I admire your honesty!" Gwen replied. "I mean, the only way I know how to get syrup is by pouring it straight out of Mrs. Butterworth's head!"

The girls hiked in silence for a little while, each mulling over how they'd tap the sap once they found the trees. If they ever found the trees...

But just when Vanessa was ready to tell her group that she would happily take control again, Reese called out, "LOOK!"

Straight ahead was a glorious grove with leaves, just like the one pictured on their map.

"We found 'em!" O'Ryan said triumphantly.

"Well, how can you be sure these are the right maples?" Vanessa asked, looking at the five-pointed leaves. "The park is filled with them."

"Look-it," Oki said, pointing to the tree trunk. "Would a regular old tree have a faucet and bucket attached to it?"

"Groooooovy!" Gwen said, running over to the tap and twisting it like she was turning on bath-water. "And—look—there's plenty of sap in the bucket already."

There were just a few drips at first, and then— "Neato mosquito!" Gwen laughed as droplets of sap dripped from the tree.

"Okay, quick, who has a cup to collect the sap in?" Yvette asked.

The girls all looked at one another. No cups?!

"Here!" Gwen said excitedly, taking her Happy Trails hat, "use my cap as the cup!"

"Uh, nice of you to offer, Gwen, but what if we want to use the syrup later?" Vanessa replied. "It would taste like your head!"

"So maybe we should put it in one of Oki's suede shoes," O'Ryan teased, "'cause she has pretty sweet feet."

"Hardee-harr-not-funny," Oki replied.

"Hey!" Yvette said, reaching into her knapsack and pulling out the sandwich she'd brought for lunch. "We can use the Ziploc bag I packed my hot dog in. Hold my dog, puh-lease," she said to Vanessa, as she cupped the plastic baggie under the sap tap. "Okay, now let the love flow," Yvette added.

Once the girls had filled the bag with what they eyeballed to be a cup of sap, Vanessa nodded and looked at her watch.

1:26 P.M. – 34 minutes left

"Okay, team," she said, "we only have one task left after this, so let's take four minutes to eat. Everyone ready for lunch?"

"Born ready!" Gwen replied. "Let's picnic."

When Oki looked at the muddy ground, though, she rolled her eyes. She didn't want to sit down and mess up her skirt. Then she remembered the "creativity kits" that Mrs. P. had given them!

In each kit was a garbage bag…

A garbage bag that could be fashioned into a picnic blanket!

"Cool," Oki said as she sat down, now perfectly protected from mud.

She invited everyone to pile on her blanket and start eating, which they did—everyone, that is, except Gwen, who'd already eaten her lunch for breakfast!

"Drat!" Gwen said. "Looks like I'll be picnicking in mime."

"Here, Gwen," Reese said, "have my apple."

"Thanks, but no thanks," Gwen replied. "Apples aren't quite sweet enough for me."

"Bet it would be sweet enough if you added maple syrup!" Vanessa suggested.

Well, quicker than you could say "sugar rush," all the girls scrambled off their garbage-bag blanket to run back to the tree. But in the bucket at the base of the tree, the girls discovered that the sap wasn't sugary sweet. In other words, it was still just bland bleck—so dipper beware!

Then, just as planned, at exactly 1:30 P.M.—with just 30 minutes left on the clock—Vanessa grabbed **Groovy Girls Group Envelope #3**.

But just before Vanessa could open the clue card, the clouds opened up. And as the rain started falling in buckets, Team Groovy feared their chance to make up time was about to go slip-sliding away.

Chapter 5

Pick Up Sticks

1:33 P.M.

"Quick, quick, get under," O'Ryan said to Oki as the girls put on their rain ponchos.

Rain ponchos?

Wait. The girls hadn't *brought* rain ponchos.

But as soon as the rain started falling, Reese's first thought after, *AHHHH, WE'RE GETTING WET!* had been *AHHHH, WE NEED TO DO SOMETHING TO STAY DRY!*

And that's when the "garbage-bag rainstorm brainstorm" had hit.

"Girls," Reese had said, "poke head-sized holes in the top part of your garbage bags, then get under!"

Because Oki had already donated her garbage bag to the group picnic, O'Ryan had poked a second head-hole in the top of her bag, and ushered her friend under.

"Okay," Vanessa now said, "let's hurry up and tackle our final clue so we can get back to the bus!"

The girls had been hearing echoes of the other groups in the distance, so Vanessa not only wanted to get out of the rain, she also wanted to make sure they were staying competitive!

The final clue—in **Groovy Girls Group Envelope #3**—was this:

No camper should be without a "ritual campfire stick," or a point of origin. So please think of this tree as that point!

As you can see, there's a sign in front of the tree pointing north. If you walk due east, though, you'll find a red flag planted in the ground. (Don't do anything yet. Just keep reading.)

And in front of that flag, you'll see another sign pointing north. But north is still not the direction you want to go. You want to go west of the flag but not further than your point of origin.

Now, walk due south to find a special area that's rich with sticks.

As soon as you've selected your stick, come back to the bus where a special campfire treat awaits you!

WHAT?

"Huh?" said Gwen.

"Ya got me!" added Yvette.

"Yikes!" said Vanessa, to put a fine point on this tricky stick business.

But as soon as the Groovies dynamic map-reading duo of O'Ryan and Oki read those crazy directions, they started smiling at each other.

"Try as they might, they can't fool us!" Oki said.

"Wait, you guys *know* where to go from those instructions?" Yvette asked. "But how?"

"Yuppers! See, they're just trying to confuse us by saying we need to go east, then west. 'Cause if you think about it, that basically puts us right back here! See? It's as easy as pizza pie," O'Ryan explained, "which is the shape you should be thinking of."

Oki nodded and drew a circle showing their directional pizza compass. "Okay," she said, adding eight slices to the pie, "this pizza will show us all the directions we need to go in."

"That's one smart pizza!" Gwen said.

Oki then drew a dot in the middle of the circle. "Think of this dot as our point of origin at the tree, okay? And from the sign in front of the tree, we know which way is north, so we put that at the top of our pizza." She put a little *N* at the top to show north.

"But to find the first flag, we're supposed to go east, which is this way," O'Ryan continued, adding an *E* at the line after the second slice of the pie.

"Oh, yeah!" Vanessa said. "'Never Eat Shredded Wheat!'"

"That's right," Oki nodded, adding an S for south at the bottom of the pizza.

"But see, it says we're supposed to walk due

west of the eastern flag," O'Ryan added and drew a straight line across the middle of the circle and labeled it with a *W*. "But stop at the point of origin, which is our big dot."

"Exactly," Oki agreed. "And see from there, the directions say we're supposed to go south." She drew an arrow extending directly down from the dot. "Which puts us here," Oki said, adding an S at the bottom of the circle.

"Soooo," O'Ryan said, "as you can see from our pizza, we actually don't even have to walk to these other places at all since we already know south of the dot—where we're standing right now—is where we need to wind up!"

"That is so sneaky!" Gwen said.

"No, it isn't," Reese replied, proudly smiling at her sister and Oki. "It's just plain smart!"

"This is gonna save us so much time. Good job guys—even if you *did* have to draw yourselves a compass!" Vanessa said. "But hey, whatever works!"

And that's how, at 1:37 P.M., with a full 23 minutes to spare, the Groovy Girls Group headed—and with Oki and O'Ryan under the same garbage bag they 'two-headed"—for the finish line.

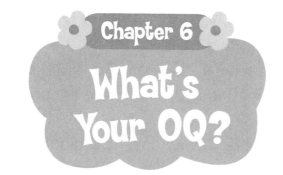

Chapter 6

What's Your OQ?

1:37:23 P.M.

"So, I actually learned something today," Vanessa said as the Groovy Girls bent over the map—one final time—to find the fastest way back to the bus.

"Don't worry, Vanessa, we won't tell anyone!" Reese replied with a smile.

"No, I'm serious," Vanessa said. "Even though I don't like admitting it, I should have listened to you guys."

"Tell us more, O wise one!" Oki giggled and smiled at O'Ryan as they got out from underneath the garbage bag they'd been sharing. Thankfully, the rain had stopped!

"You were so right about the whole map deal. It *is* really smart to make sure you know where you're going before you start going there."

"Well, now that we're talking about smart ideas," Reese said, "I think we should pit stop at the outhouse before getting back on the bus."

"Oh, goody!" Gwen agreed. "I mean, I didn't want us to lose time before, so I didn't say that I've had to go practically from the beginning."

"Okay," Vanessa said, "but we have to make it quick 'cause time is running out."

"Fine," Gwen replied. "I'll even race you all over there. Ready, set, GO!" she yelled.

Gwen took off and the other Groovies ran after her, speeding in the direction they assumed was the outhouse.

But after running full steam ahead for several

minutes, there was no sign of that little outhouse on the prairie!

"But…"Gwen said, "but I swear I remembered it was this a-way."

1:42 P.M.

"So where's the outhouse?" Yvette asked.

"Right next to that YOU ARE HERE sign," Reese said.

"Yeah," Oki said, turning around, trying to get her bearings, "but the question is 'we are *where*?'"

"Well, wherever we are," Vanessa replied, "we're eighteen minutes away from missing our bus!"

When the girls all looked at their watches, another minute had ticked off the clock.

"Make that seventeen," Yvette said.

1:43 P.M.

"I can't believe we didn't check the map before we started running. That was so dumb!" Vanessa said. "Especially after I'd just blabbed about how right you guys were to follow the map!"

"Okay, so let's just *all* look at the map together this time and see if we can figure out where we are and where we need to go," Yvette said calmly.

The girls spread the map out on the ground and zoned in on some of the places they'd been earlier in the day.

"Okay," O'Ryan said, pointing to the map, "this is where we got our sticks."

"This is the way we went toward the maple trees, and here's the wide part of the stream we crossed," Oki continued, retracing their route.

"So if we go back around this way," Reese said, "we should wind up close to the outhouse and the parking lot, right?"

"Okay, then, let's get Gwen to that bathroom," Vanessa said. "Time's running out, and if we have any hope of getting that extra credit, we should run too!"

1:48 P.M.

With their new course charted, the Groovy Girls flew through the park like hummingbirds. After five minutes of running, though, Yvette started getting that nervous feeling…that feeling you get when time's running out on a test and, all of a sudden, you think all the answers you've written down may be wrong.

"Wait!" she yelled, "are we totally one hundred percent sure we're going in the right direction now?"

As soon as Yvette said this, even the map-tastic duo of O'Ryan and Oki started having doubts.

"We're definitely going in the right direction! Trust me," Gwen shouted.

"Trust *you*? But Gwen," Vanessa said, "after all that, you didn't even look at the map with us just now!"

"Okay, so fine, you don't have to trust me. But you *can* trust Clementine!" she replied, pointing to the ground. And there,  laid out like Hansel and Gretel's trail of bread crumbs, was the path of Clementine peels Oki had discarded earlier in the day.

"See, we were definitely here before, and if we stay on this course, we'll get back in a jiff," Gwen continued, bending down to pick up the peels as she went.

"Okay, I'm convinced now," Vanessa said.

"Onwards to the outhouse!" Yvette yelled.

1:57:25 P.M.

"Ohmigosh, I feel so much better!" Gwen said, exiting the outhouse.

"Me, too," Reese said. "But I'll feel even better once we get on that bus! So now let's make like trees and leave!"

1:59:52 P.M.

With eight seconds to spare, the members of Team Groovy arrived at the bus.

"How'd we do, Mrs. P.?" Vanessa asked, huffing and puffing.

"Did you puzzle out your clues and use your map-reading skills?" their teacher asked.

"We sure did!" Reese replied.

"Then you did very well," Mrs. P. answered. "And your team came in twenty-third."

"Twenty-third?" Vanessa said. "Twenty-third out of twenty-five? We came in twenty-third??? That's as abominable as the snowman!"

"Shoot the boot!" Reese said, crossing her arms in front of her.

"Twenty-third," Oki repeated. "Well, I guess that just means we have a low O.Q."

"What's an O.Q.?" Yvette asked.

"Outdoor Quotient," Oki explained. "But at least our Fashion Quotient is high."

"Well, low O.Q., no O.Q., or whatever," Gwen said, "I still think the woods rock!"

And everyone seemed to agree, since no one wanted to get back on the bus. Fortunately, though, their adventure wasn't quite over.

"Before we head home," Mrs. P. said, "I want everyone to take their sticks and follow me." She then led the group to the main area of the park, where a campfire was burning. "Sticks out, please!" Mrs. P. added, and began to jab marshmallows onto the tips of the hikers' sticks.

As everyone warmed themselves by the fire, they began roasting their marshmallows. And whether those marshmallows were perfectly toasted, burnt to a crisp, or remained totally fluffy, everyone was happy with the end result.

And *that* was not something that needed to be checked on a map!

"That's the wrong direction," O'Ryan said to her twin.

"Nuh-uh," Reese replied, "we *want* to be facing east."

"But then, won't the sun wake us up in the morning?" Oki asked.

"Which is exactly what we want," Vanessa joined in enthusiastically. "It's a survival thing."

"Maybe that's what *you* want when you're camping out," Gwen replied. "But my survival depends on sleeping in as late as possible!"

"You know," Yvette said, taking a big sniff of fresh air, "the great outdoors has a lot to offer us."

"True," O'Ryan replied, "especially when it's located right next to the kitchen, and we can smell the cheese for our nachos melting!"

After the field trip that day, having a sleepover in the McCloud's backyard that night seemed like the only "natural" thing to do. Of course, it might have felt a little more natural had it not been so c-c-c-cold outside!

"Anyone else freezing like a Klondike bar?" Oki asked.

Reese nodded. "Maybe it isn't so smart to camp out in February," she said.

"Well, the key is layering, you know," Vanessa said, digging into her overnight bag and pulling out a woolly fleece jacket. "If you put something like this over your PJs and under your parka, you'll feel toasty as a marshmallow!"

Oki reached in her bag, but all she pulled out was a pair of tights. "This is the only extra layer thing I packed."

"You *only* brought an extra pair of tights?"

Gwen replied, scratching her head. "You always bring at least two extra outfits and a few pair of jammies to suit your mood."

"Well, maybe I learned that sometimes over-packing isn't such a smart call," Oki replied, thinking of her heavy backpack on the trail.

The girls nodded.

"Um, okay, but why two pairs of tights?" Reese asked.

"Because what if one pair runs?" Oki giggled. "But let me just tell you, I think this is going to be the first *and* last time this little camper ever packs light again!"

"Seems like Oki doesn't have such a low OQ after all!" Gwen said.

"Right," Oki replied, smiling, "and not only that, I'd know what to do if a large feathered thing came flying right at me."

"What would you do?" O'Ryan asked.

"I'd make like Daffy and DUCK," Oki yelled. "PILLOW FIGHT!" She grabbed her pillow and thwacked Vanessa with it.

As the girls thrashed, bashed, and crashed around the McCloud's yard, squealing with delight, the stars above them seemed to twinkle with an equal amount of joy.

"Hey," Reese shouted, pointing to the sky, "is that a shooting star?"

The girls put their pillows down and looked up.

"I think it's just a plane," O'Ryan replied.

"Too bad," Gwen said, "'cause I was just about to make a wish on it."

"What were you going to wish for?" Yvette asked.

"A veggie supreme pizza," Gwen replied.

As soon as Gwen mentioned the word pizza, *naturally* all the other Groovy Girls started wishing for one too.

"I think this might count as one of those walkie-talkie emergencies," Vanessa said, pulling a cell phone out of her bag. "Even though we had to give the walkies back, as team leader I'd never let my group go into the woods without the proper provisions."

After double-checking with Mrs. McCloud that it was okay to place the order (and after making sure she'd pay for the pizza when it arrived!), the girls called their fave pizza place.

But ten minutes later, Vanessa's phone rang again.

"Hello?" she said.

"Wonder who that is?" Yvette asked.

"It's the delivery guy," Vanessa replied. "Says he's new and got lost trying to find his way here. He's wondering if we can give him directions."

The Groovy Girls smiled at one another.

"Sure," Reese said. "Ask him if he has a map!"

"And tell him to use it!" Gwen added.

Each Groovy Girl had a suggestion for the delivery boy—which landmark to use, which way to turn—and each wanted to make sure he was properly oriented.

After all, the girls knew he too was playing a version of "Beat the Clock." If he didn't deliver the pizza in thirty minutes or less, he'd have to give them the pie for free. But even though the Groovies liked the idea of free pizza, they liked the idea of giving him perfect directions even better!

"Tell him to go two blocks east of the river!" Oki shouted.

"And north of the grocery!" O'Ryan added.

As the girls continued calling out directions, they knew one thing for sure: being together at the sleepover was definitely where *they* were meant to be!

Groovy Girls™
sleepover handbook

SLEEP-OUT SLEEPOVER
Great Ideas for a PJ Party Under the Stars

FUN WAYS TO SPEND TIME IN THE GREAT OUTDOORS

Be a Trail Mix Master:
Delish Snacks to Take on the Trail

Chicks Rock

Groovy Girls®

Contents

Text by Julia Marsden
Illustrations by Bill Alger and Yancey Labat

A Groovy Greeting

HEY, GROOVY GIRL!

We're gearing up for the Great Outdoors—and some awesome fresh-air adventures—but before we head out, I want to clue you in to all the cool stuff that's going on with us.

For starters, there's our extra adventure-packed hike—and our first-ever backyard sleepover. Check out pages 4–5 for our cool campout sleepover ideas. Maybe you'll want to assign each of your guests a role, like games specialist, song leader, or arts & crafts director, or just plan on everybody doing their part to make your sleepover a naturally groovy gathering.

Check out pages 8–9 for clues on staging the coolest outdoor treasure hunt ever. And you won't want to miss lots of great ways to make crafts, using seriously cool supplies provided by Mother Nature herself. (Who knew pinecones could be so much fun?)

Whenever we get together, you *know* we can't get enough of scrumptious snacks—and this time is no exception. We're serving up some of our fave recipes on pages 12–13: including all the ingredients you'll need to become a trail mix master!

With all our crazy outdoor antics, you may be wondering how you and your friends would measure up in the Great Oudoors. Put yourself and your buds to the creative test with some of the imaginative ideas on pages 14–15.

And remember, whether you choose to stage your sleepover under the stars or inside with tents and sleeping bags—you'll always be a natural wonder!

Till next time, stay true to your amazing self!

L.Y.L.A.G.G,
(Love You Like a Groovy Girl)

Gwen

GEAR UP FOR A GREAT OUTDOORS SLEEPOVER

What could be cooler than spending the night under the stars with your friends? Invite your buds over for a backyard sleepover (or create a cool campsite right under your own roof). Wherever you decide to set up camp, pitch a tent and prepare for all-out fun!

Send out invites that clue in your guests to the sleepover theme. Each note can take shape as a tent with flaps that open to reveal the sleepover 411. Or the invites can be shaped like a marshmallow, a moon, a star, a hiking boot, or a compass.

You're Invited to a Great Outdoors Sleepover!

Pitch a tent or two—inside or out. Pop-up tents work well. If you're setting up camp inside, you can always create a temporary tent by clearing off a tall table (to allow for head room in case you're sitting up in your sleeping bag) and draping bedsheets over the top of it. Or arrange several high-back chairs in a triangle or square pattern with room between the chairs for a few sleeping bags. Then, drape a bedsheet over the chairs.

Invite the outdoors in by playing a nature soundtrack. Take a tape recorder outside to your backyard or a local park and record the sounds of birds singing, rain falling, wind blowing, or crickets chirping. Or choose a soothing sound such as a babbling creek from a white-noise machine or from an alarm clock that features nature-sounds.

Start with glow-in-the-dark star stickers.
Or create cut-out stars from fluorescent card stock,
using a star-shaped cookie cutter or a free-hand
star drawing as your pattern. You can place the
stars on large black poster board and use tape
to position them on your ceiling or windows, or
on the inside of your tent for a starry sky sleepover.

Gather some naturally cool decorations from outside such
as maple leaves, pine tree clippings, and handfuls of pinecones.
Arrange them on tabletops or raised surfaces around the
room where you'll be sleeping.

❀ Ask your folks if you can bring any large houseplants from
around the house into the room where you'll be setting up the
sleeping bags. If your family has an artificial Christmas tree or
garlands, wreaths, swags, or sprays, ask if you can use them
to add some outdoors to the scene.

❀ Consider draping a strand or two of white, glimmering
lights around the room to sub for starlight.

Add some wildlife to the party by placing stuffed animals
(your favorite rabbits, bears, and squirrels) around the room.

Munch on energy bars, trail mix,
toasted marshmallows, hot dogs, and
hamburgers. Hand out a long stick to
each guest for roasting the hot dogs and
marshmallows (just like the Groovy Girls do).
Serve juice or soda from sports bottles or canteens.
Check out the recipes on pages 12–13.

Plan to sing some goofy campfire songs such as "John Jacob
Jingleheimer Schmidt," "On Top of Spaghetti," and "100 Bottles
of Pop on the Wall." Hand out harmonicas for a real 'round-the-
campfire vibe (or consider kazoos for a super-silly sing-along).

HAVE A FIELD DAY!

Plan on plenty of awesome outdoor party games! Here are a few fun activities to try:

Set Up an Outdoor Scavenger Hunt

Hand out a plastic or paper bag to teams of two or three friends, along with a list of outdoor items for them to find. Examples include: a yellow leaf, something purple, a small stick, a feather, a seed, a gray rock, something straight, something round, and something rough. Set a time limit. The team that finds the most objects first wins. Prizes could include mini flashlights, clip-on compasses, or whistles.

Take a Sock Walk

Each girl should grab a pair of old white or light-colored socks and slide them over her shoes. Go for a walk in an area with lots of tall, overgrown weeds and grass. Once you've covered some ground, pull out a magnifying glass for a close-up look at all the seeds and other stuff you've picked up while on your hike. Award prizes to the girls whose socks end up with the weirdest or prickliest or most colorful attachments.

Count Yourself in for Three-Legged Soccer

You'll need at least four people to play. Pair up in teams of two. Standing side by side, use a pair of old nylons or a scarf to tie your center legs together at the ankle and at the upper thigh. Play soccer using the regular rules. Shorten the length of the field if only a few people are playing.

Friendship Q and A's

Whether it's a sleep-out sleepover or a "follow the leader" friend, here are some answers to your friendship queries.

Outdoors Sleepover

My friends are planning an out-doors sleepover. I'm kind of nervous about spending the night outside. What should I do?

Overnights spent under the stars are a little different from indoor sleepovers. Strange noises, chilly temperatures, and that light-of-the-moon scene can be unsettling. Packing smartly can help. A portable stereo with a headset can "tune out" unfamiliar sounds. Dressing in lots of layers (think T-shirts and leggings layered with sweats, or pajamas and a bathrobe with a coat on top!) will keep you warm, and having a flashlight can help shed light on the dark. Outdoor sleepovers can always start outside and then move back inside when it's time for some shut-eye.

A "Following" Friend

One of my friends is always turning to me when it comes to making decisions. She doesn't seem to be able to make up her own mind and—unlike the Groovy Girls—it's starting to get on my nerves. How can I let her know how I feel without hurting her feelings?

First off, realize that she's probably turning to you because she likes you and wants to be more like you. The thing is, she may not have the same kind of confidence in herself. Rather than coming down on her, tell her that you think she comes up with great ideas and makes great decisions on her own. You may find that's all the encouragement she needs to speak her mind!

10 TERRIFIC TREASURE HUNT TIPS

Map out an awesome activity by planning a too-cool treasure hunt. Whether you use a compass, creative inspiration, or group consensus to find the loot, it's likely to be a rewarding experience!

1. Decide whether the treasure hunt will be for a single group or for teams. (If you want to take part in the treasure hunt, an older sibling or an adult should create the map and clues.)

2. Pick a great location. Your treasure hunt can be in your backyard, somewhere in your neighborhood or at a local park, or a nearby field. Just make sure all the players know the boundaries of the treasure hunt area before things get underway. Also, let players know if there's a time limit to the treasure hunt. If there is, be sure each team has a watch and that everyone starts at the same time.

3. Get creative with your treasure hunt clues. You can write riddles, compose poems, or use drawings. Each clue should lead the players to the next point on the treasure hunt map, and once there, they should find another clue that will lead them to the next spot.

Here's a sample poem clue:

Roses are red, lawn chairs are blue, step near the garden hose to find your next clue.

4. Create a cool treasure map on white computer or construction paper using colored pencils. Tear the edges of the paper to make the map look ragged and old. Then rub the front and back of the map with a damp, used tea bag to give it an aged appearance. The paper will take on a light brown "antique" look. Crumple the map in a ball and let it dry overnight. The next day, unrumple the map and it will look like an ancient treasure map.

5. Plan on having as many clues as there are players. Each stopping point can have a clue that's written up for a particular player to solve so that everyone who's playing has a chance to solve a clue on her own. The last clue leading to the treasure can be one that everyone solves together.

6. Consider a compass treasure hunt. Getting oriented is the secret to steering you toward the treasure. Hand out a compass to each player or team. Then provide clues such as "Stand below the oak tree. Take 20 steps west."

7. Make every step count. Create a map based on the number of steps players need to take in various directions to reach the stopping points on the map.

8. Snap to it with a photographic map that's made up of Polaroid pictures or images from a digital camera that provide the visual clues of the treasure hunt locations.

9. Listen up to clues that are snippets of song lyrics that have been recorded on a cassette tape, or listen to a cassette of someone guiding you with words to treasure hunt locations.

10. Have the players discover delicious loot at the end of the hunt as the treasure.

NATURAL WONDERS

Go for some naturally groovy accessories and create make-it-yourself memories of your own outdoors adventures. Here are some fun projects to get things started.

No-Sew Sachets

Re-create the scent of the Great Outdoors.

What You Need:

* Two 5-inch fabric squares
* Craft glue
* Potpourri made from outdoors stuff, such as lavender, pine needles, small pinecones, rose petals, rosemary, thyme, basil, sage
* Ribbon or yarn

What You Do:

1. Place two fabric squares back-to-back and glue the edges together on three of the four sides. Spread the glue close to the edges to help prevent fraying. Let dry.

2. Once the glue has dried, fill the fabric square with about 1/2 cup of potpourri. Then glue together the open side, and let dry.

3. Stack a few sachets and tie them together with a pretty ribbon or piece of yarn.

To Make Potpourri

Gather a collection of fragrant flower petals and leaves, such as lavender, rose petals, mint, rosemary, and thyme leaves. Place them on a sheet of paper and let them dry. To make a finer potpourri, when the flowers and leaves are completely dry, grind them up by placing them in a zip-top plastic bag and using a wooden rolling pin to crush them. To make a more fragrant potpourri mix, you can add a drop or two of essential oil of lavender or rose from a craft store.

Naturally Beautiful Bracelet

With a flip of a wrist, you can show off tiny treasures you've collected while exploring the Great Outdoors.

What You Need:

* Construction paper strips

* Clear packing tape

* Special flowers, leaves, clover, seeds, and feathers you have collected

What You Do:

1. Before you and your friends head out on a hike, wrap your wrists with clear packing tape, sticky side out.

2. Decorate your packing-tape bracelet with seeds, leaves, clover, and flower petals you collect along the way—placing the stuff you choose face-down on the tape.

3. Once your creation is complete, cover up the small bits of nature you've collected with a strip of construction paper that's the same width as the packing tape (or use a wider strip of construction paper and then trim it to fit the width of the clear packing tape). Flip over the strip so your sealed-in findings show, and loop it around your wrist as a bracelet.

Pinecone Pets

Look to nature for a low-maintenance portable pet.

What You Need:

* Pinecones in assorted sizes

* Various pods, seeds, small twigs, bark, small nuts, and acorn caps

* Craft glue

What You Do:

1. Use the pinecones to create woodland creatures. Glue a small pinecone to the top of a larger pinecone to make a head and body. Add pinecone scales for ears and a twig for a tail to create a cute creature.

Trailblazing Treats

If hunger hits when you and your buds are exploring the Great Outdoors, just bust out one of these yummy snacks from your backpack!

Snacks On-the-Go

When you're outdoors, snacking should be all about high-energy foods that are easy to carry with you. Firm fruits such as apples, pears, and oranges are great to carry along. And for a blast of instant energy, nothing beats a tasty trail mix.

Tropical Trail Mix

Ingredients:

1/2 cup dried papaya pieces
1/2 cup dried mango bits
1/2 cup dried pineapple slices
1/2 cup banana chips
Coconut flakes
Utensils: Large mixing bowl, measuring cups, wooden spoon, zip-top sandwich bags

What You Do:

1. Mix all the ingredients in a large bowl.

2. Place the mixture in a zip-top plastic sandwich bag.

S'mores Trail Mix

Ingredients:

1 cup graham cereal such as Golden Grahams
1/2 cup milk-chocolate chips
1/2 cup mini marshmallows
Utensils: Large mixing bowl, measuring cups, wooden spoon, zip-top sandwich bags

What You Do:

1. Mix all the ingredients in a large bowl.

2. Place the mixture in a zip-top plastic sandwich bag.

Cranberry Crunch

Ingredients:

1/2 cup dried cranberries

1/2 cup raisins

1/2 cup almonds

1/2 cup peanuts or other nuts

Utensils: Large mixing bowl, measuring cups, wooden spoon, zip-top sandwich bags

What You Do:

1. Mix all the ingredients in a large bowl.

2. Place the mixture in zip-top plastic sandwich bags.

(For added crunch, consider adding 1/2 cup of sunflower seeds, pine nuts, or pumpkin seeds to the mix.)

Campfire Cuisine

Whether you opt for outdoor cooking at a campsite or backyard grill, or take things inside to a kitchen, be sure you have an adult on hand to help with the cooking detail!

Spiral Dog on a Stick

Skewer a hot dog on a long wooden stick and then wrap a stretched and flattened piece of refrigerated biscuit dough around the hot dog. Roast the dough-covered hot dog over the fire until the dough is golden brown on the outside and the hot dog has been heated through.

Indoor S'mores

Ingredients:

Fudge-covered graham crackers

Marshmallows

What You Do:

1. Place one or two large marshmallows between two fudge-covered graham crackers.

2. Smoosh together and enjoy!

HAPPY CAMPERS!

Whether you "rock" your way across a stream, follow a trail that's got total a-peel, or just spend the day communing with Mother Nature—and the down-to-earth girls you call your friends—let your imagination guide you to a great time.

Fun Ways to Pass the Time in the GREAT OUTDOORS

❀ Wear a Whistle

Whistle along to campfire songs. You and your friends can also make up a way to communicate, such as using a one-blast code for "Look" and a two-blast sound for "That's cool."

❀ Shine a Little (Flash) Light

Play charades when it's dark and use your flashlights to showcase the player whose turn it is to act things out.

❀ Accessorize with a Bright Bandanna

Twist a bandanna to create a headband. Wrap it around your wrist as a bracelet, or wave it around like a flag. What else can you think of to do with a bandanna?

❀ Fold Up Some Foil Squares

Foil can be used to wrap up a potato, create popcorn packets or serve as a cooking surface for grilling. But why not hand out some pieces of foil to each guest and see what types of mini animal sculptures everyone creates. Then take turns guessing what animals your buds made with their foil.

✿ Find a Rock Star

Search for just the right small stone or rock to present to a pal as a friendship token. Explain to her why you chose the particular rock, such as, "I chose this stone because it sparkles just like you" or "I chose this smooth river rock because it reminds me of how steady you always are."

✿ Lost in the Woods

Picture yourself in a forest. You're surrounded by pine trees, a small stream, and a field of wildflowers. You've got some string, an extra pair of socks, and some rope. What's your plan of action? Who among your friends has the best plan?

* What will you eat?
* Where will you sleep?
* How will you spend the time until you're found?

✿ Desert Essentials

To get your brain thinking beyond your backyard, picture yourself on a desert island. Here's the sitch. You know in advance that you're going to be "stranded" for a year. You can take three items from each of the following categories with you. Go around in a circle and have each person name the things she'd choose to take with her. Find out if you and your friends will be packing up your gear in similar style.

* The three CDs I'd take with me (no iPods allowed!)
* The three books I'd want with me
* The three snack-food stashes
* The three extra items of clothing
* The three things I'd take for comfort
* The three things I'd want with me to keep me busy

Create your own Groovy Girls character online at groovygirls.com

Gwen

Reese

Oki

O'Ryan

Vanessa

Yvette